# dreams of a pencil

written by Xiaonan Zhang    illustrations by Xiaoying Cao

I am a **pencil** trapped in a drawer.

You dream up stories.

You write them down with me.

Have you ever wondered what I dream about?

I dream of adventure

far from the classroom.

Where no one will know it's me.

How fun that would be!

First, I'll go to the meadow
and water my top.

And out of my tip
a **flower** will pop!

The butterflies and bears will never guess it's me. How fun and exciting that would be!

Next, I'll make an umbrella for the fish to hide under.

Above me sits a frog
in the warm breeze.

Everyone gathers to hear the frog sing.

But no one will know it's me.

How fun that would be!

After that, I'll go to the fields to explore.

I'll hide among the **green leaves,** looking like yummy peas.

Or, I'll pretend to be a tasty **zucchini**.

In the garden, there will be a party.

Everyone will be invited.

But no one will know it's me.

How fun that would be!

After the fields, I'll go to the river by the trees.

I'll become a raft. The ants will use me to cross the river.

I could also be a paddle for a rowboat.

Birds will land and play on me.

Everyone will giggle and shout.

But no one will know it's me.

How fun that would be!

At the end of my adventure, I'll go to the sports field. I'll be a **vaulting pole** for a squirrel.

Or a **javelin** for a monkey, zooming through the air.

After everyone wins a medal,

I'll head back to the classroom.

You will use me to write the stories you dream up.

And I'll keep on dreaming.

No one knows the dreams a pencil has. Like the words on a page, my dreams can be many. But my biggest dream is to become your stories.